A Neal Porter Book

Copyright © 2001 by Yvonne Jagtenberg

Published by Roaring Brook Press
A division of The Millbrook Press, 2 Old New Milford
Road, Brookfield, Connecticut 06804. First published in
The Netherlands by Uitgeverij Hillen, Amsterdam, as *Een
bijzondere dag.*

Library of Congress Cataloging-in-Publication Data
Jagtenberg, Yvonne.
Jack the wolf / by Yvonne Jagtenberg.—1st ed.
    p.   cm.
Summary: Jack is not happy on his first day of school until
he is chosen to play the part of the big bad wolf.
[1. First day of school—Fiction. 2. Self-confidence—Fiction.
3. Wolves—Fiction.] I. Title.
PZ7.J153534 Jac 2002
[E]—dc21   2002023696

ISBN 0-7613-1747-3 (trade)
10 9 8 7 6 5 4 3 2 1

ISBN 0-7613-2855-6 (library binding)
10 9 8 7 6 5 4 3 2 1

Printed in Thailand
First American edition 2002

Yvonne Jagtenberg

Jack the Wolf

ROARING BROOK PRESS

Brookfield, Connecticut

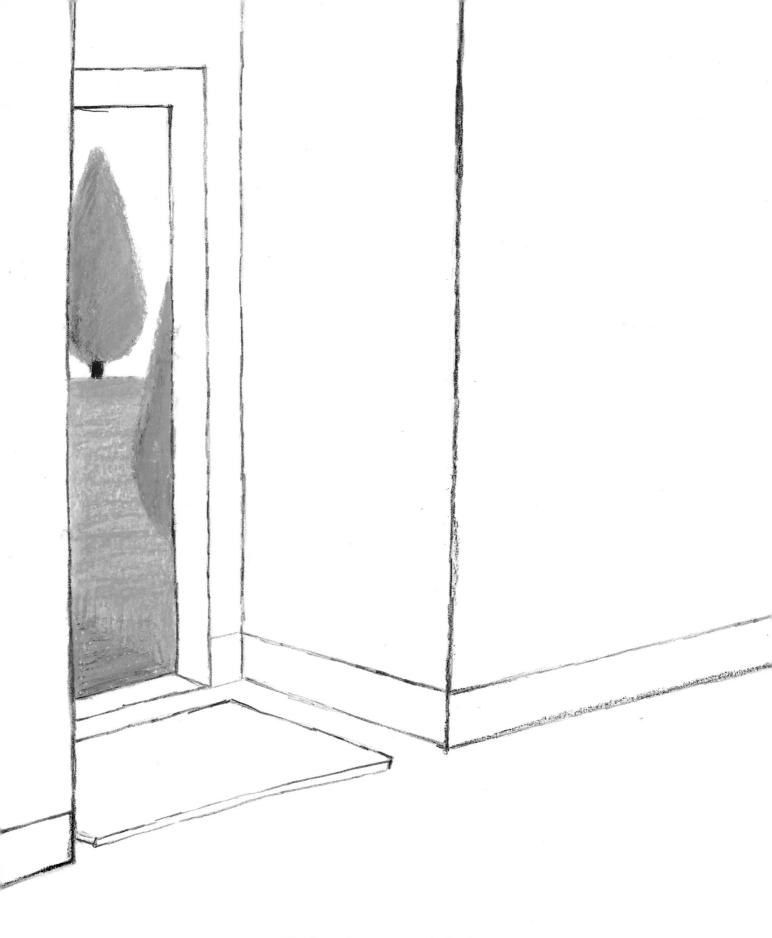

Today is a special day.
It is Jack's first day at school.

Jack is walking to his classroom
for the very first time.

Jack sees a head with pointy brown ears,
sharp yellow teeth, and a big red tongue.
Jack is a little scared.

He knocks on the door and a voice answers:
"Who's there?"

"This is Jack," says the teacher, Ms. Moody. "He is new."

All the children look at Jack.

Jack looks at all the children.

He thinks that maybe it is time to go home.

A little girl takes Jack to his seat.

She gives Jack her hand.

But Jack does not want her hand.

The children are making things.
"Why don't you make a nice chain?" says the teacher.
Jack wants to draw but is scared to ask.

It's time for gym class.
Everyone has to undress but Jack doesn't want to.
He wants to keep his clothes on.

Everyone is running.
"Run along, Jack," says Ms. Moody.

Now everybody gets a pillow.
"Throw the pillow up and try to catch it."

Jack throws his pillow on the floor.
He lies down next to it.
"Time to get up," says Ms. Moody.

"We will now sing and Jack can be the wolf today!"
The children sing: "Little Red Riding Hood,
where are you going, on your own, on your own?"

Little Red Riding Hood sings: "I'm not afraid of the big bad wolf. I'm not afraid, I'm not afraid."

But Little Red Riding Hood is afraid of the big bad wolf.

Everyone is afraid of the big bad wolf.

Jack is not.

Ms. Moody says that Jack is a very fine wolf.
Jack wants another turn.
But the other children don't want to play anymore.
They would rather play with Jack than with a wolf.

So the wolf becomes Jack again.
Soon it is time to go home.

It *was* a special day—
Jack's first day at school.